The GROTLYN

I know
when the
Grotlyn's
been,
Slipping
through
your

For EFD, who grew as this story unfolded.

First published in Great Britain by HarperCollins *Children's Books* in 2017
First published in paperback in 2018

10 9 8 7 6 5 4 3 2 1

ISBN: 978-0-00-821276-6

HarperCollins *Children's Books* is a division of HarperCollins *Publishers* Ltd.

Text and illustrations copyright © Benji Davies 2017

Visit our website at:
www.harpercollins.co.uk

Printed in China

THE GROTLYN

Benji Davies

house
unseen...

HarperCollins *Children's Books*

One night as Rubi climbed to bed
An organ's tune whirled in her head.

She heard it in the street that day,
And now it would not go away –

I know when the Grotlyn's been
Slipping through your house unseen …
But what at first we think to be,
The eye does blindly make us see.

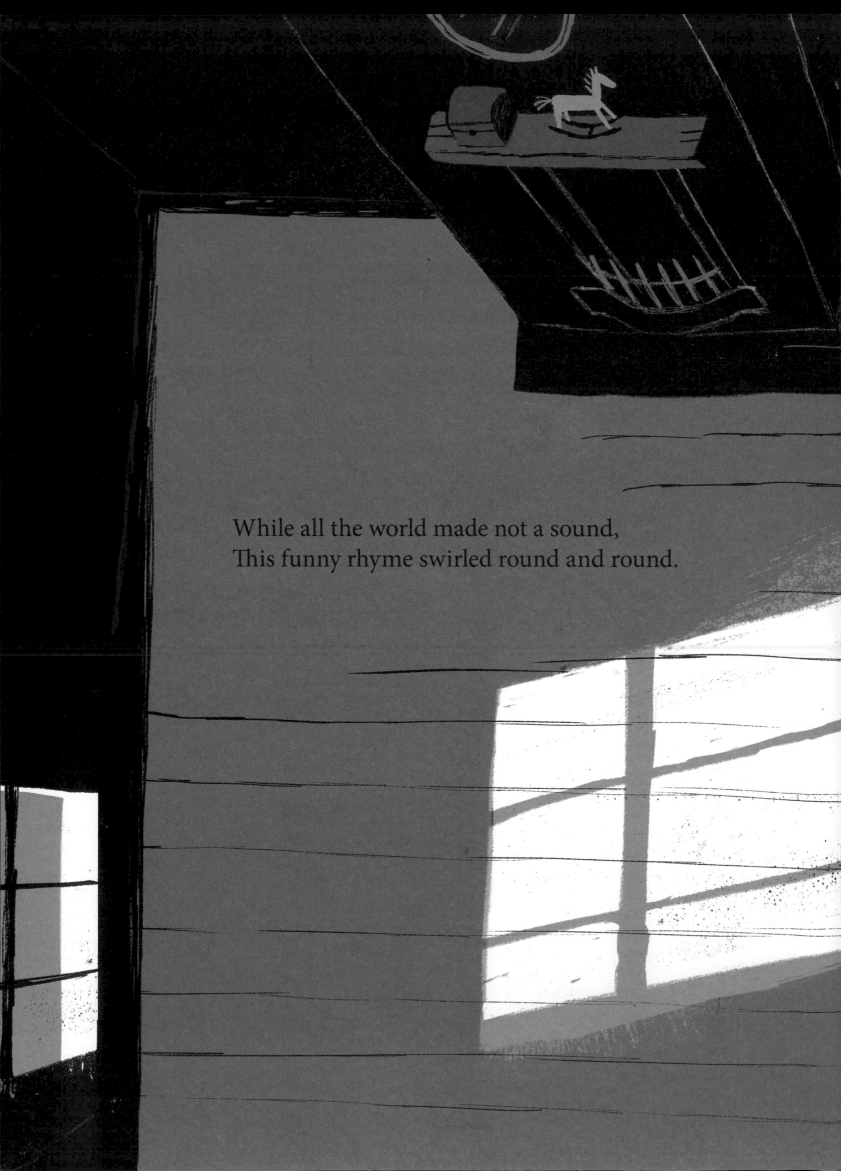

While all the world made not a sound,
This funny rhyme swirled round and round.

When nearby in the shadowed gloom,
Something scuttled through her room …

"It's just a mouse! It's just a mouse!"
she whispered to the sleeping house.

But up the
chimney,
through the
soot...

...something
stranger
was afoot.

Across the rooftops peppered black,
She hoped it wasn't coming back.

But don't be scared to sleep – to dream!
For things are not quite what they seem.

A sudden rustle – *WHOOSH* – then flap!
Sam's hair stood up beneath his cap.

"Gawd 'elp us, what on earth was that?!"
He hoped that it was just a cat.

ALCHEMY

ARCHERY

AVIATION

'Tis the Grotlyn,
plain as night!
It really gave me
quite a fright!

I think I saw it in the park –
I saw it blinking in the dark!

One night as I was
bedding down,
It scampered up my
dressing gown!

In the pantry – clear as day,
It nibbled all the cheese away!

Halfway across town,
Policeman Vickers,
Hung out to dry
his vest and knickers ...

But – *oh!* Look out! The Grotlyn's here!

"Stop, thief!" he cried without a fear.

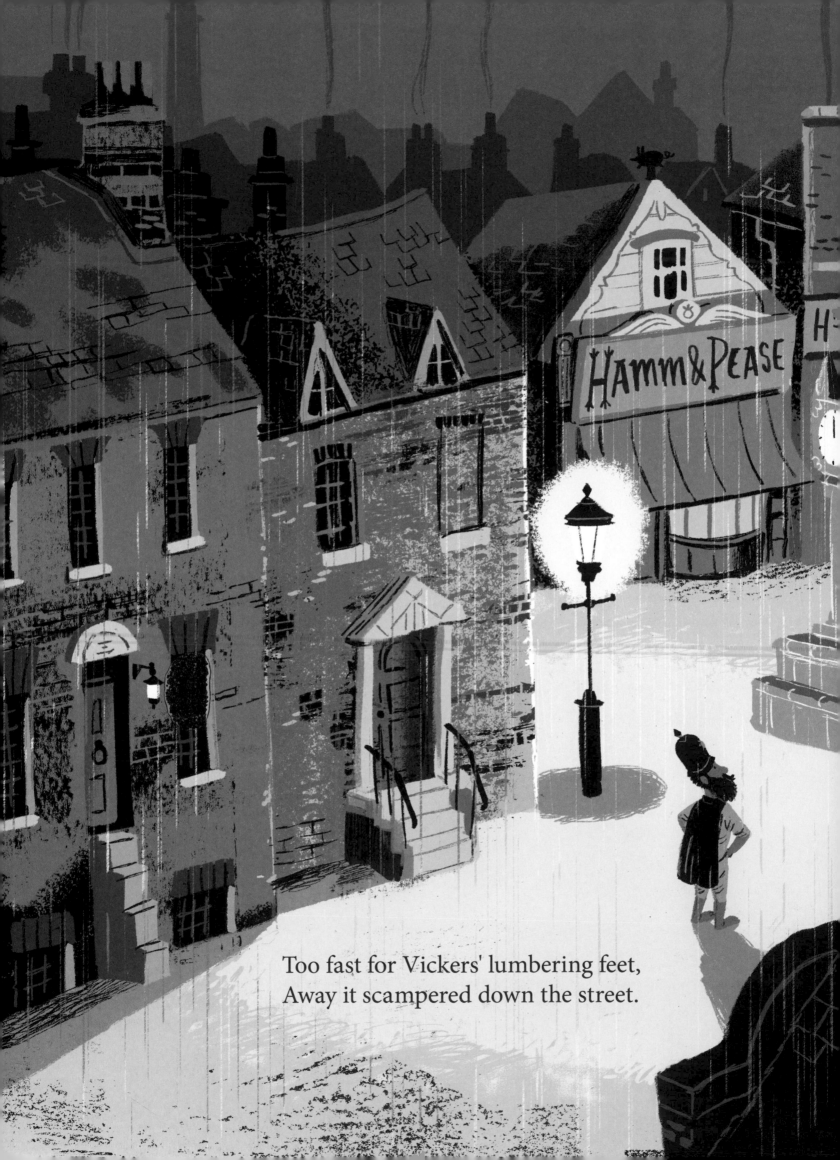

Too fast for Vickers' lumbering feet,
Away it scampered down the street.

It disappeared into the night,
Back to the shadows – out of sight!

We only know the stuff it took –
A lump of cheese, a dog-eared book,

A tin of biscuits, twisted twine,
Silk hankies from the washing line,

A length of rope, a box of tools,
An oil lamp, two cotton spools,

A basket and a wheel in tandem –
Could it be these things weren't random?

As if this thing was planning … making …
Building something – not just taking.

Cutting cloth and bending wires,
Swift with scissors, needles, pliers.

Casting knots and tying bows,
Weaving thread it neatly sews.

For what at first we think to be,
The eye does blindly make us see.

This secret plan bound for the skies –
A hot-air-filled balloon surprise!

What young Rubi heard that night –
A monkey simply taking flight.

The things he took, that little ape,
Were borrowed for a grand escape!